Michael, thank you for your endless love and support.
H. C. & L. May your hearts always be filled with love, kindness, inclusion, and joy. –R.M.

For my dearest husband and five sweet children. –D.P.

Rosalie Mastaler

Danelle Prestwich

HUNTER'S TALL tales

"Can I *please* stay home?" I asked.

"A new school can be scary,
but you are brave.

Besides, I know how much you
love school, *and* recess
will be a lot of fun."

Mom squeezed me so hard I thought my guts might spew out.

"I love you," she said. "From the top of your head down to your five little toes."

I dragged my feet down the street.
My toes teetered on the edge of the curb.

I stopped to watch a
green grasshopper hop.

I looked for animal shapes in the clouds.

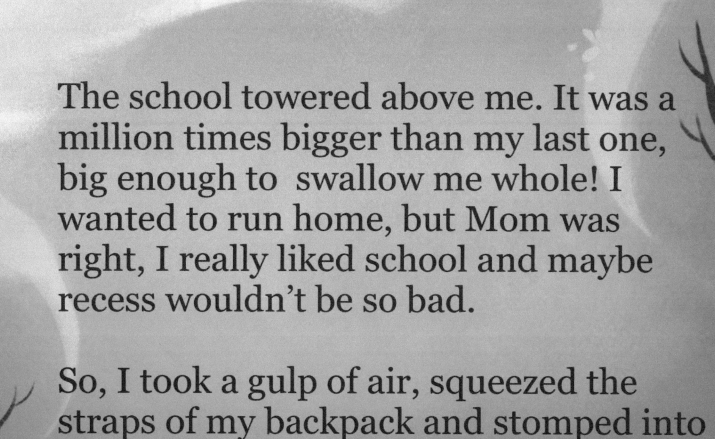

The school towered above me. It was a million times bigger than my last one, big enough to swallow me whole! I wanted to run home, but Mom was right, I really liked school and maybe recess wouldn't be so bad.

So, I took a gulp of air, squeezed the straps of my backpack and stomped into the belly of the beast. I can do it.

I tried to sneak into the classroom, but my teacher spotted me and helped me find my desk. Sometimes, I wish I had a button to make myself invisible.

The girl behind me wouldn't stop staring at my prosthetic leg. I could see the questions boiling in her brain getting ready to erupt out of her mouth like gushing, red-hot lava!

"What's wrong with your leg?" she asked.

Here they come . . .

"Is it broken? It looks like metal," she said. "Is it a robot leg or something?"

"Yeah, I'm part robot. I get it from my dad's side of the family."

RING Lunchtime!

My tummy rumbled while I waited in line. I couldn't tell if it was because I was hungry or full of nervous butterflies.

I wanted to hurry and sit down, because the boy behind me was invading my space.

"What's up with your leg?" the boy said.

"When I was little, I didn't eat enough vegetables. So, my leg didn't grow."

The boy rushed past the chocolate sprinkle cake and held out his tray. "Peas, please!"

Finally, the best time of day—*recess*.
The swings are my favorite.

I watched a girl's eyes follow my legs
back and forth, back and forth.

Here come more questions in 3 . . . 2 . . . 1 . . .
"Why is your leg like that?" she said.
"It looks weird."

"I have three pet piranhas:

Smiley

Goldie

and
Fred.

Sometimes I go swimming with them. But, one day, I forgot to feed them and they got hungry. They said my leg tasted good."

I jumped off the swing,
ran towards a soccer ball and kicked it as
hard as I could. It almost touched the clouds!

The ball bounced and rolled right behind a boy.

"Hey, do you want to play soccer?" I asked.

"Sure. I'm Miles." He looked down at my leg, and then up at my face.

Here we go again. MORE questions . . .

"What's your name?"
Miles asked.

Did he just ask my name?

"I'm Hunter!"

"Can you kick the ball with that leg?" Miles asked.

"Yeah! I lost my leg a long time ago, so I've had a lot of practice. I've kicked the ball at least a hundred times."

We passed the ball back and forth and all of a sudden, a whole bunch of kids were playing with us.

On the way home, I hopped over cracks,

raced the school bus down the street,

and zoomed up my driveway.

"Hi, Hunter! How was your day?"
Mom met me at the door
with a smile.

"So good!"

She hugged me so tight,
again. This time I was sure
my guts would spew out.

"Want to play in the backyard?" Mom asked. "I'll bring you your favorite snack."

"Yes, please! And don't forget extra for Smiley, Goldie, and Fred."

A portion of the proceeds from *Hunter's Tall Tales* will be donated to assist Hunter in attending camps, adaptive sporting events, and other opportunities to connect with the disability community. Thank you for your support and contribution!

A Note to the Reader

This is my son Hunter, the inspiration for *Hunter's Tall Tales*.

When Hunter was young, I would take him to the park and always noticed when kids stared at him. They would often ask, "What happened to your leg?" As a young child, Hunter would feel awkward and uncomfortable when kids would pay attention to his leg and nothing else. One day, a child approached Hunter and asked, "Hey, do you want to play?" Hunter perked up and ran off to play. At that moment, I realized the importance of inclusion. Questions can sometimes feel isolating, but invitations to play and friendly greetings can help a child feel a sense of belonging and inclusion.

Inclusion starts in the home, before the playground, in public, or at school. A child can better understand disabilities when they see a character in a book or on a screen and are able to ask questions in an environment where they can openly talk to an adult. Also, exposure prior to an interaction in public will almost always lead to a positive experience. I encourage you to find more books and opportunities to introduce and create awareness around disabilities.

When your child is around someone who has a disability try these few tips:

Instead of **"Don't stare,"** try **"What do you see?"** This question can open up a conversation and you can add something along the lines of: **"I'm so glad you see them!"** or **"Their body looks different from yours, and that's okay."**

If your child asks about a mobility aid such as a wheelchair, prosthetic leg, or walker, a simple reply could be, **"They use wheels to get around,"** or **"That is a prosthetic leg. They use it to walk."** And follow it up with **"Isn't that cool?"**

Lastly, try not to hush, shame, or separate your child from someone with a disability. If they are saying something negative, steer them in the direction of saying something positive. Positive language when talking about anyone's body should always be encouraged.

It's never too late to teach inclusion. And don't worry about saying the wrong thing. You've got this. I am rooting for you!

Sincerely, *Rosalie*

Rosalie loves to tell stories that open windows and doors for children to see beyond the world that surrounds them. She also finds joy when children see themselves in books and are able to say, "Hey! They look just like me!" She advocates for disability visibility by creating entertaining children's literature and ultimately hopes to help kids understand the meaning of inclusion and friendship.

Rosalie was born and raised in Southern California, but currently lives near Austin, Texas with her awesome husband and three rambunctious boys.

For more works from Rosalie check out *Represent! Vol. 1: 30 true stories of trailblazers, artists, athletes, and adventurers with disabilities*. And don't forget to visit her website where you can find *The Ultimate Book List*—one of the largest databases of books that feature characters or real people with disabilities.
www.RosalieMastaler.com

Oh, and hopefully social media will always be a thing, so go to @mastalerpartyof5 for some entertaining videos of things like Hunter walking on LEGO without even a flinch.

Danelle enjoys bringing stories and characters to life through her art. She has a Bachelor's of Fine Art in Illustration from Brigham Young University—Idaho.

She spends most of her time at home raising her five young children. On occasion they are mistaken for a herd of wild animals, but please be reassured that they don't bite—often. Danelle spent her childhood in the suburbs of Cincinnati, Ohio and currently resides with her family in Albuquerque, New Mexico.

Text © 2023 by Rosalie Mastaler
Illustrations © 2023 by Danelle Prestwich
All Rights Reserved. Printed in the United States of America

Published by Motina Books, LLC, Van Alstyne, Texas
www.MotinaBooks.com

Library of Congress Cataloguing-in-Publication Data:
Names: Mastaler, Rosalie & Prestwich, Danelle
Title: Hunter's Tall Tales
Description: First Edition | Van Alstyne: Motina Books, 2023
LCCN: 2023902730

ISBN-13: 978-1-945060-58-8
ISBN-13: 978-1-945060-57-1
ISBN-13: 978-1-945060-59-5

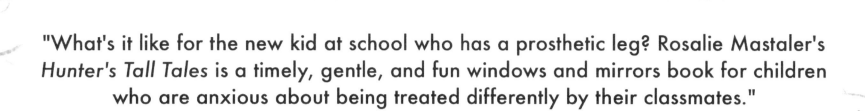

"What's it like for the new kid at school who has a prosthetic leg? Rosalie Mastaler's *Hunter's Tall Tales* is a timely, gentle, and fun windows and mirrors book for children who are anxious about being treated differently by their classmates."
-NANCY CHURNIN, Award-Winning Author of *Martin & Anne, and Dear Mr. Dickens*

"*Hunter's Tall Tales* is a delightful, fun, and humorous read that raises awareness about differences while modeling compassion, kindness, and friendship. This book is a wonderful way to open up a conversation with young children about inclusion as they continue to learn about the world around them."
-AILEEN WEINTRAUB, Author of *We Got Game! 35 Female Athletes Who Changed the World*

"*Hunter's Tall Tales* is not just a book for those of us born or who look different, but a relatable book for all, giving the message to never stop being YOU."
-ALEX BARONE, Actor, and Community Outreach Coordinator for No Limits Foundations

"*Hunter's Tall Tales* is a fun story for kids of all ages that weaves together playful illustrations with silly responses to that never ending question, 'What happened to your leg?' As someone who has responded to this very question with my own tall tales, I can relate to Hunter's encounters with his curious classmates!"
-JOSH SUNDQUIST, Bestselling Author, Speaker, and Halloween Enthusiast

"*Hunter's Tall Tales* is full of color, whimsy, and magically imaginative moments."
-DANNY JORDAN, Author, *The Capables*

CPSIA information can be obtained
at www.ICGtesting.com
Printed in the USA
LVHW012016300623

751264LV00004B/129